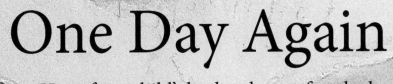

One Day Again

~Hope for a child's broken heart after the loss of a loved one~

Written by Rebecca Wilson
Illustrated by Graciela Herrero

Published by Yawn Publishing LLC
2555 Marietta Hwy, Ste 103
Canton, GA 30114
www.yawnspublishing.com

Library of Congress Control Number:2020924624

ISBN:978-1-947773-97-4 Paperback
        978-1-947773-98-1 Hardcover

Printed in the United States of America

Preface:

The little bird in this book is a reflection of the Holy Spirit in our lives. He shares with your child the promised hope of God's redemption in our lives and our world. This promised hope can be experienced even in the throes of grief. From the beginning of the story, he acknowledges the initial tear-filled feelings of loss and then goes on a quest into what we should know and rest in as Christians. The bird's flight brings him back, full circle, to a scene reflecting relief and comfort, which is my hope for the child reading this book.

A helpful process to grieve is to recognize the loss tangibly. There is a special place in this book. I encourage you to have your child add a picture of their beloved, whether human or animal. Give your child a pencil and let them write a memory or hope for *One Day Again*. If they can't write, then help them. They can draw the picture.

"Let not your heart be troubled: ye believe in God, believe also in me. In my Father's house are many mansions: if it were not so, I would have told you. I go to prepare a place for you. And if I go and prepare a place for you, I will come again, and receive you unto myself; that where I am, there ye may be also."
~John 14:1-3 KJV

"Grief is something that hits us all and this book speaks to this, especially as it affects the heart of a child. This book will go a long way to soothing the broken heart of a child with the promises given to us in the Bible. Please share it with your child, over and over again."
~Ebb Fox, Lead Pastor, Calvary Chapel Woodstock, Kennesaw, GA

"Any loss is a great loss to a child, and many parents feel uncertain about how to help their children heal after losing someone they love. This book speaks to children in language they can understand and gives them hope, the antidote to grief, and a salve to heal their broken spirits."
~Heidi Moore, MD Pediatrician and Author, Waleska, GA

"The book, *One Day Again*, provides an amazing connection for children who are suffering the loss of a loved one. Being an educator in a private school, I would share this book with my students and suggest it to my colleagues and those suffering from grief."
~ April McDonald Hammond, 2nd Grade Teacher, St. Augustine School, Lebanon, KY

"Positively filled with love and light. A balm for the broken hearted."
~Mindie Leigh Carter Henry, Hospice Coordinator, Surf City, NC

He knew he had to say goodbye,
the thought of it made him cry.

He hung his head, closed his eyes,
then he heard a little bird sigh…

In the window up above
strangely sat a small white dove.

Of all the things he thought he knew,
a bird speaking, was this true?

Here is the encounter the little bird told
of a flight He took to a city of gold…

He went on and on about treasures that were there,
and the tales of these sites He remarkably shared.

His was the experience of the animals that…

had been loved on Earth
and now ran and sat…

...in fields of wildflowers and fescue hay,
in ponds full of lily pads in the lovely warm shade.

He sang of the love, so much to spare,
and of pain and suffering that no longer was there.
Take a deep breath and rest easy my dear,
it's all of these promises that you need to hear…

Our Father in Heaven loves us so much,
He gave us a way to once again be in touch.

It should settle your sadness and give you some cheer
to know your beloved will one day again be near.

For now we must trust in Christ Jesus
and give Him our hearts,
then we can be assured of our salvation
and in Heaven, never be apart.

In those moments there was relief,
a brand new hope, a new belief.

The loss of his beloved was real,
but he knew the promise was sealed.

He said a thankful prayer with amen
because he believed in one day again.

God will give us a land where everything is new;
this is the land where our little bird flew.

My story about
One Day Again

The Author: Rebecca Wilson grew up in Lexington, Kentucky, and now lives on a small farm in the foothills of the Georgia Blue Ridge Mountains. She loves the Lord, her family, and all her farm animals. She homeschools her two boys and has been married to her boyfriend for twenty years.

The Illustrator: Graciela Herrero is originally from Uruguay and now lives in America. She loves God and all of His creation. She lives with her dog and her cat and is very close to her two grown boys. Graciela's God-given passion for art made her a sculptor and an illustrator.

A note about this book:

I wrote this book for you to have a way to comfort your child whose heart is devastated during a time of loss. Read it together to open a dialog. Be bold in your assertion; we WILL see each other One Day Again! You need to know this for yourself as well, and if you are not convinced, I am praying now as I write this that God gives you direction to the scripture that comforts your heart and gives you His confidence in these matters. I've listed a few scriptures in the back of the book that helped me. It is not the end of the story. The time we have had here with our loved ones, even pets, is just an introduction to the beautiful life in eternity for those who are believers in God and His Kingdom to come.

The beginning of my writing process for this book came about when a little girl I know and love, Andi, experienced her pet's death. Andi's baby goat, sadly and unexpectedly, died. Upon hearing from her mother that my young friend was having a tough time, I went to find a book to give her as a gift. I searched for one that gave a biblical perspective to help with her grief. There were books about the death of cats and dogs, but nothing about goats. If you look for her in this book, you will see her holding Lucky the goat.

On other pages, you see people depicted representing someone I, or my illustrator, Graciela, know or have known. The opening page shows a boy with his head hung and shoulders heavy with grief. This image was originally a photograph that I took of my son just before the vet came to our farm the day our dog Max died. As a mother, I wanted to take away the grief he was experiencing, but I could not. Instead, I captured the photo so that I would never forget his pain. I needed to hold on to it. In suffering, we can count on God to bring healing. Maybe this book will bring someone healing, and that was why I anxiously took that picture long ago.

Also captured in the illustrations is a beautiful little girl in a white dress whose name was Sierra. She is with her dog, Rocco. She had Down syndrome and cancer on this earth, but now, she is healed, reunited with her best pet, and whole in mind and body in Heaven. Her sweet mama will see her, *One Day Again*. There are other special people in this book as well; those stories were just a few of many. Please know the intention of this book is founded on loss but published in hope. My goal is to project the great hope and anticipation for what is next because it will be glorious.

We must trust the Holy Spirit to soothe our pain with His promise of what is next, just like the little bird does in this story. God bless you and your child, and know that I have prayed for you both as I have prayed over this book. I feel my heart connected to children experiencing grief and the parent who mercifully wants to take that burden from their child. In its most infantile suggestion, couldn't that be what Jesus felt for us on the cross?

In His service,
RW

"But seek ye first the kingdom of God and his righteousness, and all these things shall be added unto you."
(Matthew 6:33, KJV)

"And God shall wipe away all tears from their eyes; and there shall be no more death, neither sorrow, nor crying, neither shall there be any more pain: for the former things are passed away." (Revelation 21:4, KJV)

 "But the Comforter, which is the Holy Ghost, whom the Father will send in my name, he shall teach you all things, and bring all things to your remembrance, whatsoever I have said unto you. Peace I leave with you, my peace I give unto you: not as the world giveth, give I unto you. Let not your heart be troubled, neither let it be afraid." (John 14:26-27, KJV)

But as it is written, Eye hath not seen, nor ear heard, neither have entered into the heart of man, the things which God hath prepared for them that love him. But God hath revealed them unto us by his Spirit: for the Spirit searcheth all things, yea, the deep things of God. For what man knoweth the things of a man, save the spirit of man which is in him? Even so, the things of God knoweth no man but the Spirit of God. Now we have received, not the spirit of the world, but the spirit which is of God; that we might know the things that are freely given to us of God."
(1 Corinthians 2:9-12 KJV)

"If ye then, being evil, know how to give good gifts unto your children, how much more shall your Father which is in heaven give good things to them that ask him?" (Matthew 7:11 KJV)

CPSIA information can be obtained
at www.ICGtesting.com
Printed in the USA
BVHW021040080222
628387BV00007B/512